STRANDED

STRANDED

JANNETTE LaROCHE

DARBY CREEK
MINNEAPOLIS

Darby Creek
An imprint of Lerner Publishing Group, Inc.
241 First Avenue North
Minneapolis, MN 55401 USA

For reading levels and more information, look up this title at www.lernerbooks.com.

Image credits: MihailUlianikov/Getty Images, (crystals); Master3D/Shutterstock.com, (winding road); Hans Neleman/Getty Images, (car); Tom Hurst / EyeEm/Getty Images, (background); kovop58/Shutterstock.com, (backpack); alexandre zveiger/Shutterstock.com, (sweatshirt).

Main body text set in Janson Text LT Std 12/17.5.
Typeface provided by Adobe Systems.

Library of Congress Cataloging-in-Publication Data

Names: LaRoche, Jannette, author.
Title: Stranded / Jannette LaRoche.
Description: Minneapolis : Darby Creek, [2020] I Series: Road trip I Summary: "When Kevin and Jesse get stuck in the middle of the woods on their way up to a family cabin, their weekend takes a turn for the worse. How will the boys make it to safety?"— Provided by publisher.
Identifiers: LCCN 2018044265 (print) I LCCN 2018050637 (ebook) I ISBN 9781541557024 (eb pdf) I ISBN 9781541556867 (lb : alk. paper)
Subjects: I CYAC: Survival—Fiction. I Adventure and adventurers—Fiction. I Forests and forestry—Fiction.
Classification: LCC PZ7.1.L355 (ebook) I LCC PZ7.1.L355 Str 2020 (print) I DDC [Fic]—dc23

LC record available at https://lccn.loc.gov/2018044265

Manufactured in the United States of America
1-46120-43495-6/26/2019

For my Hamlettes

CHAPTER
1

Jesse pulled up to the curb in front of
Kevin's house to find him already waiting.
At least, he assumed that was Kevin. All he
could see of him were a bulging backpack,
a pair of army boots, and sturdy-looking cargo
pants. Kevin's face was barely visible between
the sleeping bag and tackle box squeezed in
his arms. He looked like he was prepared for
a trek into the jungle rather than the long
weekend at Jesse's cabin they had planned.

Jesse cracked a smile as he popped the
trunk for Kevin to load up his gear. When
everything was stowed away, Kevin climbed
into the passenger seat and they took off.

"What's all the stuff for?" Jesse asked as he followed the line of traffic out of Kevin's neighborhood to the main highway.

"Camping," Kevin said, grabbing a cookie from the pile of snacks sitting between the front seats.

"You know we have a cabin, right?" Jesse asked. "You didn't need your sleeping bag."

Kevin shrugged. "I thought we might want to sleep outside."

Jesse shuddered at the thought. He loved going to the cabin. But he loved it in the same way he loved any vacation: done comfortably. And with beds.

"So, what exactly are we going to do this weekend?" Kevin asked.

"We can do anything we want. When I go up with my brother we usually just hang out and watch TV or play games."

Kevin laughed. "That's what we do basically every weekend. I was hoping to do something more outdoorsy since we will be, you know, in the woods."

"We share a lake with a few other cabins,

so we can go out on the boat or do some fishing. And there are hiking paths, if that's more what you were thinking," Jesse offered without much enthusiasm.

"That sounds great," Kevin said. He paused thoughtfully before adding, "Before we moved here we lived about half an hour from a state park. My dads and I used to go camping—like, in-a-tent-with-no-running-water kind of camping—practically every other weekend from spring to fall."

Jesse was surprised he didn't know this about his friend. He hadn't really thought much about what Kevin's life used to be like before he had moved to town at the beginning of the school year. The two were in most of the same classes together, they both played on the soccer team, and they even went to the same synagogue. They became friends pretty fast. But Kevin had never talked much about his past. Jesse had assumed it had been pretty much the same as it was now.

No wonder he was so excited to go on this trip, Jesse thought. *But he's going to be disappointed if he thinks I'm going to spend all weekend doing that nature stuff.*

"I guess we could do a few things outside," Jesse agreed. "Usually when I go to the cabin I'm just looking for an excuse to get away from my parents so I can do what I want and eat as much junk food as humanly possible."

"You'll change your mind once we get there," Kevin said.

Jesse just shook his head. He didn't plan on it. Kevin had never seen the cabin: the awesome game system set-up, the massive TV that was even bigger than the one Jesse had at home, the fridge still stocked from his last trip up with enough food to last through the weekend. Once they got there, Kevin would be the one changing his mind.

"We're lucky the weather is good," Jesse said. "What are the chances of it being so warm right when we have a long weekend?"

"I hope you're right. I saw there's a small chance of rain later tonight," Kevin replied.

Jesse smiled at the thought of the weather cooperating with his weekend plans of staying inside and gaming as much as possible. As soon as they were all set up in the cabin, it could pour the whole rest of weekend, as far as he was concerned.

**

After almost two hours of driving, Jesse pulled into a rest stop so they could stretch their legs and grab some more road snacks.

Kevin watches as Jesse got three mini bags of chips, two candy bars, and a packet of beef jerky out of the vending machine. "You are serious about those plans to pig out this weekend."

Jesse grinned through a mouthful of chocolate. "This is just for the last hour of the drive," he said. "Once we get to the cabin I'll show you my stockpile."

Jesse offered a bag of chips to Kevin, who shook his head and laughed. "I think the half a bag of cookies I've already eaten will tide me over until dinner, thanks." But he shoved his own wrinkled bills in the vending machine and bought a couple of bottles of water.

Jesse held back a laugh. *Leave it to Kevin to pick the only healthy option in the vending machine,* he thought.

"Why don't you drive the rest of the way," Jesse suggested when they got back to the car. "That way I've got more hands for snacking."

"Are you sure?" Kevin asked. "Your dad won't mind?"

Jesse's parents had helped him buy his car when he turned sixteen. But even though the car was technically Jesse's, his dad was super strict about making Jesse take very good care of it. He had a rule that no one other than Jesse was supposed to drive.

Then again, his dad also had a very strict no-eating-in-the-car rule. Jesse was going to have to destroy all evidence of their car snacks before he got home. But, for now, they were on vacation. And vacation meant having fun.

"What my dad doesn't know can't get me grounded." Jesse grinned as he tossed Kevin the keys.

Kevin got behind the wheel and spent a lot of time adjusting the mirrors and making sure he could find the lights and wipers. Then he backed out of the spot slowly and headed for the main road, checking that he was clear to turn three times before easing onto the highway. Jesse rolled his eyes but didn't say anything.

Kevin was just starting to look comfortable behind the wheel when they hit a traffic jam.

The car slowed to a stop behind a long line of red brake lights.

"I hope it's not an accident or something," Kevin said.

"I just hope it clears up soon," Jesse said. He was impatient to get to the cabin.

**

Unfortunately, Jesse did not get his wish. After over half an hour of stop-and-go traffic, they'd only moved a mile.

"This is ridiculous," Jesse sighed. "There's an exit coming up soon. We can take the back way. My family does it all the time."

"I don't know," Kevin said. "I looked at the map before we came and this highway seems like the best way to get there."

"Does this look *best* to you?" Jesse pointed at the traffic creeping slowly along for as far as they could see. "Trust me. I've been going to this cabin my whole life. I know these roads like the back of my hand."

Kevin chewed on his lip. "Maybe the traffic will clear up soon."

"I'll make you a deal," Jesse said. "If we're back to normal speed before we get to the exit, we'll go on. Otherwise, we'll go my way."

Twenty minutes later, they turned off the highway and onto a small, gravel country road.

CHAPTER 2

With each passing landmark—the weird blue barn, the old school bus that had been on the side of the road for as long as Jesse could remember, the billboard advertising a diner where the waitstaff all wore ridiculous hats—Jesse felt his excitement grow.

"We ate there once," he told Kevin, pointing to the billboard.

"Did you have to wear hats too?" Kevin asked.

Jesse laughed. "They had paper hats that were supposed to be for the little kids, but my dad insisted the whole family put them on. His barely fit on his head, but he was so happy with himself. We probably took a hundred pictures. It was hilarious."

At the time, Jesse had been totally embarrassed, but his dad wouldn't take no for an answer. And they'd ended up actually having fun. Jesse smiled to himself as he gazed at the scene passing outside his window. But his smile faded as he realized he didn't recognize the area anymore.

"Hold up. I think we missed our turn."

Kevin scowled at him. "I thought you knew these roads like the back of your hand."

"I guess I don't look at the back of my hand that much," Jesse said with a grin.

Kevin was not amused. "Are you absolutely sure you know where we're going?"

"Just turn around. We can't have gone too far past it."

Jesse was right. They'd only missed the turn by a mile. But he felt a lot less sure of himself now. It was true that his family had taken this back way before, but not for years. Ever since construction on the highway had finished the summer he turned ten, they'd pretty much only taken the back roads as a last resort. And when they did, Jesse hadn't paid much attention from his position in the back seat.

Jesse pulled out his phone. The signal was faint—spotty reception was pretty normal for these back roads—but he still managed to call up a map of the area. The little blue dot showed him where they were. He zoomed it out to see where the cabin was, then back in, working his way backward from the cabin along the smaller roads to the one they were on now. He put his phone away and started paying close attention to the roads they were passing.

"The next street is called Timberlane, and it will be on the right," Jesse said. "And then we take a left on Mantruth."

They found the first road exactly where Jesse predicted, but Kevin still didn't seem to fully trust Jesse's navigation skills.

"It looks like it could rain any time," Kevin said. "How much longer do you think we'll be on these back roads? The highway seems safer if there's a big storm."

Jesse groaned. "Then we could end up sitting in a traffic jam for hours out in the open. That's no better."

"I'm not saying we should go back," Kevin said quickly. "I'm just worried about the weather."

Kevin kept driving.

"I think that's it there," Jesse said when he saw a gap in the trees.

Kevin slowed down so they could see the sign clearly. Mantruth Road.

Jesse's relief at finding the street was short-lived. The road was narrower than he remembered and the trees were so dense they often reached across the road, blocking out what little light was still shining down. It was like the beginning of every horror movie set in the woods.

As if to complete the picture, a bolt of lightning suddenly shot across the sky, and it started to rain.

"It's not far now," Jesse promised. "We stay on this until we go over a bridge. And then we turn onto a small road on the left. We'll see a little clearing right before we have to turn so we can't miss it. And that's the last road before we reconnect with the highway."

Kevin shook his head slightly. "I'm really not sure about driving in the rain like this," he said. "I don't want to mess up your car. Why don't you drive?"

"I have to navigate," Jesse said. "You're doing fine."

In truth, Jesse was probably even more scared than Kevin was. But not because he was worried about the car. This last stretch of road always terrified him. The trees grew even denser and dropped so many leaves over the ground that it could be hard to see if you were staying on the road. He hated that part, even when his dad was driving in good conditions. And he wouldn't call what was happening outside *good*. The rain was picking up, and the sun was already down past the tops of the trees and sinking farther each minute.

Kevin eased the car over the bridge and continued along the road, slowing down so much at any sign of their turn that Jesse wasn't sure he was even touching the gas pedal. Finally, they passed the clearing and found the road, exactly as Jesse had described. It was also as scary as Jesse remembered—a packed dirt road, scattered with leaves and debris, that wasn't even wide enough for two cars to pass each other. Trees towered over the road from both sides, turning it into a dark tunnel that seemed to go on forever.

All of his childhood fears came back to him. Despite everything Jesse had said before, he would rather spend another five hours in this car than drive on this road. In the dark. In the rain.

"Let's go back." Jesse's voice was little more than a whisper.

"Now?" Kevin asked. "You said we were almost there. Besides, this was your idea."

Kevin had him there.

Kevin drove slowly at first, but the road wasn't as bad as it looked and he soon picked up speed. And then he slammed on the brakes. The car slid to a stop only feet from a tree that lay across the road.

Jesse swore under his breath. Kevin was breathing hard, and his hands were shaking. He took a couple of deep breaths before he spoke. "Let's take a look. Maybe we can move it enough to get around."

"No." Jesse said. "You were right earlier. We should have turned around before. Now I'm agreeing with you, and that's two-to-zero in favor of going back around the long way."

"But I'm changing my vote," Kevin argued. "So it's one-to-one again. And by your logic, since you *didn't* want to go back before, it's really zero-to-two."

"That's not how this works," Jesse insisted. "Besides, it's dark now and it's starting to rain for real."

"How about we rock-paper-scissors it?" Kevin suggested.

Jesse thought about this for a minute. But apparently Kevin was only joking. Without another word (or a rock, paper, or scissors) he got out of the car and started walking around the tree.

With a sigh, Jesse stepped out onto the cold, wet, dirty road and went to help.

"I think we need to have one person push at this end while the other pulls it from over there," Kevin said, firmly standing at one end of the downed tree and pointing to the other.

Jesse went to the opposite end and wrapped his arm around a thick branch. He tried to get a good grip as pine needles poked at his face and sap soaked into the sleeve of his windbreaker. Kevin counted to three and Jesse pulled as hard as he could. After a few

seconds, the tree did start to move, but all it
did was roll slightly to the side.

"Maybe if we both pull from the same side
we can get better control," Jesse suggested.

But the tree still wouldn't move. After
pushing and pulling for a few minutes, they were
no closer to getting the tree out of their way.

"I guess we're back to the long way
around," Kevin said.

Jesse wasn't quite sure who held the rights
to say *I told you so* in this situation. He wanted
to be the winner of the argument. It didn't
really matter, though. They were both very
wet and very cold and they had a very long and
miserable drive ahead of them. It seemed to
Jesse that neither of them had really won.

Kevin had left the keys in the car and Jesse
slipped into the driver's seat, knocking the mud
off his shoes as best he could before pulling his
feet in after him.

As soon as Kevin was in, Jesse started
to back up. He cranked the wheel as far as
it would go, but the road was so narrow he
barely turned at all. He cranked the wheel

the other direction and stepped on the gas. The wheels spun for a second, then suddenly gained traction and the car surged forward.

Right into the downed tree.

CHAPTER
4

Jesse let out a sound that was half-rage and half-terror. He jumped out to check on the damage and Kevin followed. There was a huge dent in the bumper. Jesse bent down to look closer but between the rain and the dark, he couldn't manage to see much of anything.

"Oh, man," Kevin said. "I can't believe that just happened."

"I know," Jesse groaned. "My dad is going to kill me."

"I'm sure he'll understand. It was obviously an accident."

Jesse let out a short, bitter laugh. "You've met my dad. You know what he's like. Remember how he freaked out that time he thought there was a scratch on the door? Even when he found out it was only a streak of mud, he was still angry at me for a week for letting it get so dirty."

Kevin tried a different tactic. "He can't blame you for Mother Nature, right?"

"Oh, trust me, he'll find a way to make it my fault. I should have stayed on the highway. I should have checked the weather first. I should have put chains on the tires."

"You have chains for your tires?" Kevin asked.

"No, but Dad will probably say I should. Once he's made up his mind about something, he refuses to believe anything else. He's the most stubborn person I know."

Jesse saw the corners of Kevin's lips twitch.

"What?" Jesse demanded.

"Nothing," Kevin said. He took another look at the bumper as if maybe it had magically fixed itself while they'd been standing there in the rain. "You can tell him I was the one driving," he offered quietly.

Jesse shook his head. "He'll be even angrier at me for letting you drive. He won't blame you, though. He made it very clear when I first got it that anything that happened to this car would fall one hundred percent on me."

Jesse got back into the car, not even bothering to scrape the mud off his shoes this time. He couldn't really get into any more trouble than he already was in.

"Look on the bright side," Kevin said as he joined him. "It's not like this day could get any worse."

Jesse put the car back in reverse and worked his way back, turning as much as possible. Then in drive. Then reverse. Back and forth. Back and forth. But he hardly made any progress turning around.

And then the car wouldn't move at all. Kevin got out and looked at the tires.

"The road is mush," he reported. "Your wheels are dug into about six inches of mud. There's no way we're getting out of here tonight."

"Well that's just great!" Jesse folded his arms across the steering wheel and rested his head on them. "What are we going to do now?"

"I guess we're going to have to call for help," Kevin replied. He pulled out his phone and stared at the screen.

"Yeah, about that . . ." Jesse said. He realized he probably should have mentioned the spotty signal thing earlier.

"We could walk back to the other road. Maybe we'll get a signal there?" From the way Kevin said it, Jesse could tell he didn't have much hope of that working. And he was right.

They were stuck.

"The next time I start to say something can't get any worse, please slap me," Kevin said.

Jesse grinned. "Oh, you can count on it." But the smile didn't last long. He sighed. "We'll have to sleep in the car. By morning the road might be dry enough that we can get out. If not, we can push it out. I guess for now we should dry off as much as possible, change clothes, and have something to eat."

Even that was easier said than done. They grabbed their things out of the trunk, doing their best to block most of the rain with their bodies as they took their bags into the main part of the car. Kevin pulled out a towel, which quickly became wet and dirty. Still, they managed to get most of the water out of their hair so it wasn't dripping into their eyes anymore.

Then they grabbed their pajamas from their bags, but changing in the car was awkward. Jesse slammed his elbow against the window more than once as he worked the wet clothes off and the clean, dry ones on.

Jesse fished out the rest of his vending machine haul. But they only had one of Kevin's bottles of water left.

They ate the rest of the snacks and each took a sip from the water bottle. Then they settled in for the night. Kevin pulled his sleeping bag out of its sack and offered it to Jesse, but Jesse refused. There was no way he was going to make his friend uncomfortable when Kevin was the one who'd actually been prepared.

Jesse reclined the driver's seat as much as possible without squishing Kevin, who was lying across the backseat. Jesse was cold and uncomfortable. He was sure he would never fall asleep. Kevin didn't seem to have the same problem. He started snoring in about five minutes.

The forest wasn't as quiet as Jesse would have expected. Without the solid walls of the cabin around him, every sound seemed unusually loud. The rain grew stronger, battering against the roof of the car, then gradually coming to a stop. The wind moving through the trees made a strangely comforting rustling sound. Jesse heard an owl's hoot, and footsteps of animals skittering on the ground and in the trees.

Jesse realized this was probably much closer to what Kevin had been expecting out of this trip than what he had been hoping for himself.

CHAPTER
5

The next morning, Jesse woke up stiff and cold, but mostly hungry. It actually wasn't the first time he had woken up. He felt like he hadn't slept more than ten minutes at a time all night. But when he opened his eyes this time the sun was up enough to make it worth staying awake, even though he couldn't see much yet.

Jesse started the car, not even bothering to wake Kevin up. All he could think about was getting someplace that opened early for breakfast. But the tires spun even worse than the night before.

"What's going on?" Kevin asked sleepily.

"The car still won't move." Jesse banged his fist against the steering wheel.

Kevin opened the back door. "Oh man," he said.

"What?" Jesse asked. "What's wrong now?"

"You're not going to like this," Kevin replied.

Jesse snorted. "Of course not. Just tell me what's going on."

"You know how we're on a road? Well, now there's also a stream that wasn't there last night. I think maybe the tree is trapping the water."

"Trapping it where?" Jesse asked. But he was pretty sure he already knew the answer.

"Trapping it in the middle of the road," Kevin confirmed.

Jesse rolled down his steamed-up window and looked at the muddy mess where the road should have been.

I will not cry. I will not cry.

Jesse kept repeating the words in his head until he was sure he could control himself. They were stuck in the middle of nowhere.

No one knew where they were. They had no way of calling for help. And there was very little chance of anyone coming by this way and finding them—because of course no one would be stupid enough to take this road when the ground was wet like this.

He almost thought, *What else could possibly go wrong?* but gave himself the mental slap he warned Kevin about earlier. For some reason, Jesse was pretty sure they were about to find out exactly what else could go wrong.

"Okay, new plan," Jesse said.

"Great, let's hear it," Kevin said.

"Actually, I was kind of hoping you had one," Jesse admitted.

"Any chance your phone is working?" Kevin asked. They both pulled out their phones, but they were still no good.

"How far would you say we drove on this road last night before we got to the tree?" Jesse asked.

"Two or three miles," Kevin guessed. "Not more than five for sure."

"That makes things more complicated,"

Jesse told him. "It means there's at least twenty more miles until we would have connected back with the main road on the other side of our detour. So we have to decide whether to go the long way toward the cabin or head back to the gravel road the way we came, where there's a better chance we'll come across a car or someone sooner."

Kevin considered for a minute. "The road is in such bad shape we probably won't be able to walk on it. That means we'll have to go into the woods, which will slow us down. But we'll still get to the gravel road a lot quicker than continuing on the long way."

I guess Kevin is going to get his hike in the woods after all, Jesse thought.

After they got dressed, Kevin asked Jesse for his backpack. Jesse handed it over to him and Kevin dumped the contents of both of their bags out onto the backseat.

"Hey!" Jesse protested.

"We need to take a few things with us," Kevin explained. "But we don't want to be weighed down with full bags."

Kevin started repacking the bags. He added the mostly full water bottle and the empty one to his backpack and threw in a couple of pairs of socks and a T-shirt in each of their bags. Then Kevin got out and opened up the trunk. Jesse could hear him rooting around but couldn't see what Kevin was looking for back there.

"What are you doing?" Jesse asked, but Kevin ignored him and kept digging.

Jesse sighed.

Finally Kevin returned. "Give me your shoes."

"What? Why?"

"Just do it, okay?" Kevin brushed off the question in a way that clearly showed the conversation was over.

Jesse threw his shoes at Kevin with more force than was necessary. Kevin might know more about hiking and nature and all that, but this was Jesse's car and he was the one who knew the area. He didn't like Kevin taking over like this.

Kevin added Jesse's shoes to his bag, handed it over, and then motioned for him to get out of the car and follow him toward the trees. As soon as Jesse's feet hit the muddy ground, he understood why Kevin had taken his shoes. With each step he sunk a little deeper into the mud. He definitely would have lost at least one of his shoes if he'd tried to wear them. Still, he wished his friend had told him the plan rather than making the arrangements himself and treating Jesse like a child.

Once they were a few feet into the woods, the ground was firmer. They stopped to scrape the mud off their feet with some wet leaves and put back on their shoes. Then they started walking. Or, at least they *tried* to walk. But they soon found the undergrowth was so dense they could hardly move at all.

"We'll have to go farther in," Kevin said.

"But then we won't be able to see the road," Jesse shot back.

"It will be fine. We can head straight and check every ten or fifteen minutes to make sure we're still following the road."

Jesse was starting to get tired of Kevin telling him what was best. "Maybe we should go the other direction after all," he suggested.

Kevin crossed his arms and stared at Jesse. "You said it's at least twenty miles. That will take us six or seven hours—if we're lucky."

Just then, Jesse's stomach let out a loud growl as if to remind him that he hadn't eaten anything since the junk food the night before.

Great, he thought. *Even my stomach is on Kevin's side.*

Jesse didn't try to argue anymore. He just set out in the direction Kevin wanted to go. Their progress was slow. Every couple of minutes they would find their path blocked by fallen branches or thick bushes. Climbing through the woods didn't leave them much of a chance to talk, which was fine by Jesse. All he wanted was to get to the cabin and make the most of what was left of this weekend.

Once they had gone a little ways, Kevin took the first check to make sure they were following the road. He came back and nodded to Jesse, and the pair set off again. Soon Jesse was breathing hard and sweating even though the air was chilly and he only had his windbreaker. He noticed with some envy that Kevin seemed to be doing just fine.

After another ten minutes or so, they finally caught a break. They came to a part of the forest where the trees weren't as dense. The extra space between them also meant that more light could come through and there weren't as many bushes and roots to fight against.

Jesse made the second road check and everything was looking good. All they had to do was keep on course and they would be back to civilization in no time. He felt his spirits lift for the first time since they'd turned onto that stupid dirt road last night.

"Do you hear that woodpecker?" Kevin asked.

Jesse heard a loud, fast tapping sound coming from above them. He looked up and saw the bird at work.

"I didn't know there were woodpeckers around here," Jesse admitted.

Kevin laughed, but not in a mean way. "Then it looks like you've got a lot to learn."

As they continued on, Kevin pointed out other birds he recognized, either by sight or by their calls. He named some of the trees and plants too. Jesse was impressed. He knew what poison ivy and poison oak looked like, but he'd never cared enough to learn anything else.

When it came time for the next road check, Kevin pulled out the water bottle, took a small drink, and handed it to Jesse before he headed off. As Jesse watched him push his way through the trees toward the road, he couldn't help but smile. He found himself almost enjoying the unexpected hike. Jesse drank a giant swig of water while he waited for Kevin to come back.

He waited. And waited.

Finally, he heard a shout in the distance much farther to the left than the direction Kevin had gone several minutes before.

"Here!" he called back.

Kevin crashed through the trees. When he reached Jesse, he looked shaken.

"The road . . ." he croaked out. "It's gone."

CHAPTER
6

"Gone? What do you mean?"

"I went to check on the road and it wasn't there," Kevin said in a shaky voice. "I kept going, looking all around, going deeper, but I couldn't find it."

Jesse stood very still. *This is not happening,* he thought. *We are not lost in the middle of the woods without cell reception.*

"We must have veered away from the road after the last check," Kevin said.

Jesse's temper flared. "See? I told you we should have gone the other way. If you'd listened to me, this never would have happened."

Kevin snapped back. "And if you hadn't

insisted we get off the highway in the first place, none of this would have happened. But you always have to have it your way, don't you?"

"That's not true!" Jesse yelled.

Kevin gave Jesse a look that made him feel about two inches tall. He let out a quiet, mocking laugh and walked away.

If Kevin had yelled back, Jesse could have stayed mad. But the silence was worse. It meant that he couldn't argue his way out of what Kevin had said. All Jesse wanted was to have a fun weekend. He'd had everything planned out perfectly. But now Kevin was calling all the shots and they were stuck in the middle of the woods. Jesse was so frustrated he wanted to cry or punch something. Or maybe both.

***

Once he'd had a minute to cool down, Jesse hurried to catch up to Kevin. He found him a short distance away in a clearing. The ground was dry in the sun, and Kevin was sitting and staring at his feet. Jesse sat down a short distance away. He passed the water bottle back to Kevin.

"I have an idea, if you're willing to hear it," Kevin said, taking the mostly empty bottle.

"Okay," Jesse said.

"We need to know where we are. Since we don't have our phones, you're going to have to make a map."

Jesse wasn't confident, but he finally had something to contribute to their plans. "I'll try," he offered.

Kevin gathered some sticks and rocks and Jesse used them to make a crude map of the area. He put the sticks where the roads should be, arranged the rocks as the landmarks he could remember, and drew a couple of lines in the dirt for rivers he knew were close by.

"The only problem is I don't know how accurate this is in terms of distance," he said when it was done. He pointed to one of the lines in the dirt. "I'm pretty sure about the river that we crossed before we got onto the gravel road. But this other one, I have no idea if it's five miles or twenty-five miles away.

Same thing with the roads. I'm sorry I can't remember better."

"This is really good," Kevin assured him. "At least we know we have to be somewhere in here." He indicated an area on the map. "So if we pick one direction and keep walking we'll have to hit one of these roads or a river."

"A road would be better than a river," Jesse said. "How can we make sure we stay going in the same direction?"

"The sun," Kevin said. "It rises in the east and sets in the west. If your map is right, south is our best bet. So before noon we want the sun on our left and after noon it needs to be on our right."

Jesse looked at the time on his phone. "It's almost ten o'clock right now." He found the sun and turned so it was on his left side. "I guess we go this way, then."

The boys grinned at each other. Jesse was glad they were working together instead of fighting. He made a mental note to try not to be so stubborn. It wasn't his friend's fault that they were lost.

CHAPTER
7

Jesse let Kevin take the lead when they set off
again. But it wasn't long before Kevin started
walking slower. Finally he came to a complete
stop and turned his head to one side.

"Did you hear that?" Kevin asked.

"All I hear are the trees and the birds,"
Jesse said.

Kevin looked around nervously. "I thought
I heard . . . never mind."

Now Jesse was too excited to let the subject
drop. "Did you hear a car or something?" he
asked eagerly.

Kevin shook his head and started walking
again. But he kept looking around. "Are there

bears in this area?" he finally asked.

"Just black bears," Jesse said.

Kevin grabbed Jesse's arm in a death grip. "You're just mentioning this now?"

"It's not really a big deal. I've seen maybe three or four bears in all the time my family has been coming up here, and usually it was while we were in the car. The one time we saw a bear out in the woods it took one look at us and ran the other way."

Kevin didn't look convinced, so as they walked Jesse told him what to do if he saw a black bear in the wild. Don't approach it. Raise your hands and make yourself look as big as possible. Stand your ground and yell your head off.

"I can't believe you're so calm about bears," Kevin said.

"What you really should be worried about is wolves," Jesse said.

All of Kevin's newfound confidence drained away like sidewalk chalk in the rain.

"We had a hard time with a wolf by our cabin one year."

Fear spread across Kevin's face.

"Yeah, it kept trying to huff and puff and blow the whole place down. It knocked the branches out of our tree and did some serious damage to the flowers my dad had planted."

By this point Kevin figured out that Jesse was teasing him and gave him a little shove. They both laughed and continued on their way.

***

A little while later, Kevin stopped. "Whoa! Check this out," he pointed to a trail snaking through the trees. "We should take this."

"It's not going in the right direction," Jesse pointed out. "We're headed south and this goes east and west."

Kevin looked up at the sun, which was difficult to see through the dense tops of the trees. "If we're even still headed south," he said, frowning. "At this point, I think it's more important that we cover a lot of ground than focus on what direction we're headed. Besides, if this is some sort of hiking path we'll have to run into a park or something pretty soon."

Jesse didn't know the best way forward. The trail didn't look like the ones by his cabin. It wasn't as wide or as even. And he couldn't help but notice that it looked overgrown. The trees were so close on either side that branches often stuck out right into the middle of the trail. If it were a human path, it would be much straighter and neater. Which meant the path might be an animal trail. Even though he'd been joking around with Kevin, there really were wild animals in these woods and Jesse would rather avoid them if possible. On the other hand, they'd spent the last hour or so picking their way through bushes and brambles. Following this trail would be a lot easier.

So why am I trying to fight this? Is it just because it was Kevin's idea? Jesse wondered. *Am I really as stubborn as Kevin thinks?*

"Okay," Jesse said. "We'll do it your way."

The trail was definitely a lot easier going. They still had to move branches out of their way from time to time, but they were moving much faster. Kevin seemed encouraged by their luck with the trail. He started talking eagerly. He kept saying he was sure they'd find civilization soon.

Still, Jesse was on high alert. And this was a good thing too. They'd been walking for about half an hour when Jesse heard something crashing through the underbrush ahead of them.

"Look out!" Jesse cried. He grabbed Kevin's arm and dragged them both off the trail just as something large and loud burst onto the trail.

CHAPTER
8

Seven turkeys stood pecking at the ground of the trail. They were all a lot bigger than he would have imagined, but they weren't the dangerous creature Jesse had been expecting. He peeked over at Kevin. Sure enough, his friend was covering his mouth to try to smother his laugh. He wasn't being very successful.

"You forgot to warn me about the deadly turkeys in this area," Kevin said.

"Okay, okay," Jesse said. "I may have overreacted a little bit. But I do think we need to be more careful. We don't know what other kinds of animals might be using this trail."

"Like what, chickens?" Kevin was still grinning like crazy.

Jesse wished Kevin were taking this more seriously. Ever since their conversation about the bears Kevin had been acting more and more reckless, like he had to prove he wasn't scared.

Now who's being stubborn? Jesse thought. *Or maybe just stupid.* But even though he still thought they should get off the trail, and even though he was pretty sure Kevin was making a mistake by being overconfident, Jesse kept his mouth shut.

"Let's go," Jesse said. He pushed through the tall bushes and back onto the trail. One of the male turkeys looked at him, flared its tail feathers into a giant fan, and let out a series of little yelps. The others lifted their heads and looked in Jesse's direction in almost-perfect unison. Then they all turned and darted back into the cover of the trees. The first turkey waited until the rest were gone before taking its eyes off Jesse. Then it folded up its feathers and joined its friends.

Kevin slapped Jesse on the back. "Close call there. I thought you were a goner."

"Ha ha," Jesse said dryly.

Kevin set out and Jesse followed reluctantly. Seeing the turkeys seemed to have convinced Kevin that everything was absolutely fine. It had the opposite effect on Jesse. He was twice as jumpy and nervous as before. Every time he heard a birdcall or a twig snap nearby he stopped to listen.

"Would you stop that?" Kevin asked after about ten minutes of this.

"I'm sorry, but I really don't like being on this trail," Jesse said before he could stop himself. "Maybe we could walk next to it like we did the road earlier?"

Kevin snorted. "Because that turned out so well? Besides, then all the trees and stuff would still slow us down. It would defeat the whole purpose."

"I know, I know. You're right."

Kevin sighed. "Look, do you really want to get off the path and try heading south again?"

Jesse bit the inside of his cheek to keep from yelling, *Yes!* Kevin was offering to abandon his own plan to do what Jesse wanted. Jesse couldn't help thinking this was what he was trying to do himself.

"No. We can stay on the trail if you think it's best."

"Then you have to stop jumping at every little sound," Kevin said. He looked around for a minute and picked up a large stick. It was about two feet long, thicker at one end than the other, and had little twigs shooting out all over the place. He handed it to Jesse.

"What's this?" Jesse asked.

"For protection," Kevin explained.

Jesse didn't think holding a stick was going to make him feel better, but he took it anyway. They set out again and Jesse started pulling the little twigs off the stick to make it easier to hold. As he stripped down the twigs, it also started to look a little more like a weapon—something he could use to scare off an animal if he needed to. If nothing else, the work was keeping his mind off every little sound. Kevin looked over his shoulder at Jesse's handiwork and gave him an approving nod, then continued on.

***

The longer they walked, the less the trail looked like a human-made path. In some spots, it was so narrow Jesse had to turn sideways to get through. One tree had a thick branch at head height that went right over the trail. Jesse had to duck under the smaller twigs growing out of the bottom of it. Under better circumstances, it would have made a great tree to climb.

Jesse started falling farther and farther behind Kevin as he slowly picked through the woods. He thought about calling out to Kevin to wait up, but he barely had the extra breath for it. Besides, as long as they stayed within eyesight of each other, Jesse figured they'd be fine.

He kept picking his way through the path. He got caught in a bush and had to stop to work himself free without tearing up his shirt.

By the time he managed to free himself with only minor cuts on his arms, Kevin was so far ahead that Jesse couldn't see him. He swung his stick over his shoulder and picked up speed. But he'd only gone a short distance when he heard a yell coming from farther up the trail.

What in the world is happening? Jesse wondered.

The shout came again, closer this time, and now Jesse could make out the words.

"Run! Run! Run!"

CHAPTER 9

Jesse didn't hesitate. He turned and ran back down the trail just as a frightened-looking Kevin came into view. A thousand possibilities flashed through Jesse's mind, each one more terrifying than the last.

Ahead of Jesse was the low-hanging branch he'd had to duck under. When he was a couple of feet away he threw out his arms and jumped. He managed to wrap his arms around the branch and swing his legs over so he was straddling it. He looked around for any other places sturdy enough to hold Kevin and low enough for him to reach. All he saw was his friend, only a few yards away, running like his life depended on it. Kevin was so focused on the path in front of him that Jesse wasn't sure he even would spot him on the branch.

"Up here!" he called. Kevin looked up and relief spilled over his face. Then his toe caught an exposed root and he stumbled. It took him a few seconds to steady himself.

And those were a few seconds he didn't have. A large gray animal came streaking up the path behind him, snarling.

Jesse lay across the branch with one hand gripping the branch and the other hand reaching out to help his friend climb up. *I sure hope this is strong enough for both of us*, he thought.

Kevin grabbed the tree branch, but didn't have momentum working for him like Jesse had, so he just dangled there. Jesse got a fistful of Kevin's sweatshirt and started pulling with every ounce of strength he had. He lifted his friend enough that Kevin was able to swing one leg up onto the branch. But before he could pull himself all the way up, the animal jumped up after him. Kevin screamed and nearly fell off the branch.

Jesse's heart pounded. He squeezed his legs around the branch he was sitting on so he could use both hands to haul Kevin the rest of the way up. He didn't let go until Kevin was lying on the branch, breathing hard, but safe.

Jesse quickly pulled his legs up on top of the branch and motioned for Kevin to do the same. Once they were secure, Jesse looked down. Below him, a wolf paced back and forth. Jesse inched backward, closer to the trunk of the tree where the branch was thicker and a little higher off the ground. Kevin saw what Jesse was doing and followed until they were both perched as far back on the branch as they could go.

The wolf followed the boys to the base of the tree and stretched its front paws up the bark, like it was trying to find a way to climb up after them. Standing on its back legs like that, its snout was only a few inches below the branch. Jesse was grateful this part of the tree was high enough to keep them out of reach of those terrible jaws.

Jesse took a deep breath and tried to slow his racing heart. "Can wolves . . . climb?" he gasped out.

Jesse saw the fear in Kevin's eyes as he looked down at the wolf.

"I don't think so?" Kevin's answer came out more like a question. Or maybe a wish.

They both stared at the wolf, which stared right back with fierce yellow eyes. It continued circling the tree as if looking for a way up. Its muscles rippled underneath thick gray fur as it walked. Its paws were huge, and the claws that stuck out from them looked like they could do some serious damage.

Jesse couldn't stand to look at it anymore so he turned his attention back to Kevin. "Are you all right?"

To his surprise, Kevin laughed. Or at least he made a sound somewhere between a laugh and a sob. "We're lost in the woods and a wolf has just chased us up a tree," Kevin pointed out. "I could be better."

Jesse and Kevin still had their backpacks on, but Jesse had dropped his stick when he was running. He could see it lying uselessly a little ways off.

So much for using it as protection, he thought.

"Do you think we should try to climb higher?" Jesse asked.

Kevin shook his head. "It doesn't look like the wolf can get to us here. I'd rather not risk falling if we don't have to." He took in a sharp breath as he moved his right leg into a more comfortable position.

"You're hurt!" Jesse said.

Kevin's pant leg was torn open and blood was flowing steadily down his leg, over his shoe, and dripping onto the forest floor below.

"It barely managed to scratch me. It's not that bad," he said. But the look of pain on his face gave him away.

"Let me see," Jesse urged.

Reluctantly, Kevin stretched out his right leg. He winced with each movement, and Jesse was expecting the worst. When he could reach Kevin's leg, Jesse gently pulled up the tattered remains of the pant leg.

Several large gashes extended from about halfway down Kevin's calf to an inch or so above his ankle. It was hard to see how deep they were, but they were bleeding freely.

"We need to stop the bleeding," Jesse said.

"I brought your emergency kit," Kevin said. "It's in my backpack."

"I have an emergency kit?" Jesse asked.

Kevin let out a weak laugh. "It was in the trunk. I grabbed it just in case."

Kevin tried to shift the backpack off his shoulders but started to wobble. He quickly righted himself and tried again, but the same thing happened.

"Maybe you can turn around, and I can get to it," Jesse suggested.

Kevin started to turn but almost fell for a third time.

"Stop," Jesse said. "I guess it's too dangerous to try to move around up here."

Kevin nodded, clearly happy to be able to sit still. Jesse could see that even that small amount of movement was causing him pain. But they had to get Kevin's leg wrapped up soon. Being careful to keep his balance, Jesse began to rip the fabric at the bottom of his T-shirt. When he had a good-sized piece he wrapped it around the wound. Kevin groaned, but Jesse knew he had to make it tight enough to stop the bleeding, even if it hurt.

By the time he was done, the makeshift bandage was already soaked through, but the bleeding seemed to be slowing down. The blood wasn't dripping down to the waiting wolf anymore, anyway.

"Thanks," Kevin said through gritted teeth. "Now what do we do?"

Jesse looked around for the wolf. It had stopped its pacing and jumping and was now lying directly under the boys, watching them intently.

"Now, we wait."

CHAPTER
10

Jesse went back and forth between checking Kevin's bandage to make sure he wasn't bleeding again and looking for ways they might climb through the trees and come down far away from the wolf. After what felt like the longest fifteen minutes of Jesse's life, the wolf got up and walked away like it had forgotten all about them.

Jesse waited another ten minutes until he was sure the wolf had really gone before telling Kevin they were in the clear. He dropped to the ground and helped Kevin get down so he wouldn't have to jump on his bad leg.

"Let's take a look at that emergency kit," Jesse said after making sure Kevin was seated comfortably. He was expecting a regular first-aid kit like his family kept in the bathroom at home. This one had the usual bandages in various sizes (though nothing quite big enough for a wolf attack), little packs of antiseptic wipes, antibiotic ointment, gauze, tape, and a little pair of scissors. But it also had a thin blanket, candles and matches, and a small bungee cord.

Jesse got to work taking off the makeshift bandage and examining the wound. Now that it had stopped bleeding, he could see the scratches weren't that deep, but they still looked like they hurt. He knew it was important to keep wounds clean so they wouldn't get infected.

"I wish we had some water so I could clean this," Jesse said.

"I wish we had some water so I could drink it," Kevin said.

Until that moment, Jesse hadn't remembered how hungry and thirsty he'd been since they left the car. It said a lot about the trouble they were in that he hadn't even realized how long it had been since they last ate anything.

"We'll get out of here soon," Jesse said. He was trying to comfort himself as much as Kevin.

Jesse used all of the little foil packets of wipes to clean the area as best as he could. Then he applied some of the ointment and wrapped Kevin's leg back up in the clean gauze. When he was done, he changed into the extra shirt Kevin had packed for him.

He sat back down next to Kevin. "So how much pain are you in?" Jesse asked.

"We should head south again," Kevin replied softly.

It wasn't an answer to his question, but Jesse was so surprised that Kevin had changed his mind he didn't even argue about whether Kevin should be walking at all. "Are you afraid we'll run into more wolves?" he asked.

"That's part of it," Kevin admitted. "Gray wolves live in packs. The rest of its family is probably nearby. There might be a den close to the path. If the wolf had pups that would explain why it chased me but didn't really try to hurt us."

"I'd hate to see what would happen if it *was* really trying to hurt us," Jesse said.

"We were lucky. I should have listened to you in the first place." Kevin swung his pack onto his shoulder and took off into the woods. He limped a little, but otherwise seemed to be all right.

Jesse sighed. In his effort to make up for their fight, he tried to do the right thing by not forcing them to follow his plan. But that ended up getting them into more trouble.

This is what I get when I try to stop being so stubborn, Jesse thought bitterly.

Since it was well past noon by the time they started up again, they turned so that the sun was on their right and headed off. But the deeper they went off the trail, the more difficult it became to tell just where the sun was. Twice they came to an opening to realize they had been going the wrong way. By the third time they checked, Jesse was beginning to worry that they were walking in circles.

They always seemed to be walking a little bit off from south, and he was sure they should have reached a road or at least something already. Jesse was anxious about how much longer Kevin could keep going.

"Are you sure your leg is okay?" Jesse asked Kevin. "We could take a break."

"I'm fine," Kevin said through gritted teeth.

"At least let me take the lead," Jesse said. "That way I can move the bushes and twigs out of the way for you."

Kevin muttered something under his breath that sounded to Jesse like "my own stupid fault" and picked up his pace again, making his limp even worse.

Jesse was just about to insist that they take a break—even if he had to pretend he was the one who needed it—when he heard something that sounded like traffic rushing along on a highway.

"Do you hear that?" Jesse asked. He caught up to Kevin and they stood still for a moment to listen. "Are those cars?"

Kevin shook his head sadly. "I don't think so. Let's go take a look."

They pushed through the last of the trees, and Jesse understood why Kevin was so disappointed. In front of them was not a road but a river.

"We must have been going east after all," Kevin said.

"It's okay," Jesse assured him. "We knew running into a river was a possibility. That just means that we have to follow the river, and sooner or later we'll hit a different road. Or maybe the one we were looking for all along. I'm pretty turned around at this point."

Kevin sat down. Or more accurately, he half-sat, half-collapsed, and caught himself at the last second. His face was very pale and he was sweating a lot.

"Let me check your bandage," Jesse said.

"It's fine. It doesn't even hurt anymore," Kevin insisted.

The bandage was dirty, but it didn't look like Kevin's wound had started bleeding again. Jesse had no choice but to take Kevin at his word. It wasn't like there was a lot he could do for him anyway.

But, there was.

"Give me the water bottle," Jesse said. "I'll go fill it up."

"No way. I'm not drinking river water. You don't know what kind of junk is in there. "

Jesse sat down next to Kevin and put a hand on his shoulder. "Look, we're both dehydrated. If we don't get some water in us we're going to move slower and slower."

Kevin opened his mouth as if he was going to argue, but closed it again. Jesse was sure Kevin wanted water even more than he did.

"It might be okay," Kevin said after a minute. "The river is flowing pretty fast. Standing water is more likely to be a problem." He took the water bottle out of his backpack but didn't hand it to Jesse right away.

"Is there anything we can do to make it safer?" Jesse asked.

"We could filter it," Kevin said. "But we don't have enough containers to do a good job. Also, it takes a really long time. We could do a mini-filter, though," he added excitedly.

"What do you mean?" Jesse asked.

Kevin sat up a little straighter. "Do you have the rest of that shirt you used to bind my leg?"

Jesse dug it out of his pack and handed it over. Kevin folded it over so it was four times as thick and put it over the mouth of his water bottle. Then he grabbed the other empty bottle out of his pack.

"We fill up one bottle with river water and then let it drip through the cloth into the other bottle," Kevin explained. "It won't get rid of any really bad stuff, but it will filter sand and leaves and stuff like that."

Jesse took one bottle and went to the river. He took off his shoes and stepped into the water. It was much colder than he'd expected, and the shock of it ripped through his body. But he waded out to where the current was a little stronger, figuring the faster the water, the safer they would be.

He brought the bottle back to Kevin, who tipped it over onto the one with the cloth. Even with Kevin holding them as tightly together as he could, quite a bit of water leaked out. In the end they only got about half a bottle of drinkable water. Jesse was disappointed. He wasn't sure it was worth the wasted water.

Then he saw that the cloth was covered with flecks of dirt. Jesse wrinkled his nose at the junk that he could have been drinking.

He let Kevin have that first half-bottle and then went back to collect more river water. They repeated the process several times until they'd both had their fill. Jesse's mouth didn't feel so dry anymore and, he was pleased to see, the rest seemed to do Kevin's leg some good. When they set out again, he was barely limping.

Without even asking, Jesse took the lead this time. No matter what Kevin said, Jesse knew his leg had to be hurting. Being in front was a lot harder, but Jesse was glad he could help Kevin.

***

After a while Kevin started falling behind. Jesse knew not to push the issue, so he developed a pattern. When he got too far ahead, Jesse would wait until he heard Kevin coming and then act like he'd just set to work on the bushes in front of him.

"I know what you're doing," Kevin said after about the third time Jesse had paused to let him catch up.

"What?" Jesse asked as innocently as possible.

"You don't have to wait for me. Just go ahead without me. The sooner we get to a road the better. Besides, once we do find the road, who knows how long it will take until a car comes by that we can flag down? I'd rather get there and find a car waiting with you than have you hang back with me and miss our chance."

"I don't like the idea of being separated. What if something else attacks one of us? We've made it this far because we've stuck together."

"But it makes sense to try and get to help as soon as possible."

"Well, I think it makes more sense to stay close and work as a team."

Kevin crossed his arms and scowled. Then he broke out laughing.

"What's so funny?" Jesse asked.

"We're both so stubborn."

Jesse grinned in spite of himself. "How about a compromise?" he suggested. "I'll go on and clear the way, but when I get too far ahead I'll wait until you're a little closer before I set out again. That way we can still keep moving, but we can help each other in case there's an emergency."

"Deal," Kevin said, nodding.

They agreed Jesse would call back to Kevin every few minutes. If Kevin was too far back to hear him and answer his call, Jesse would wait and try again. Feeling more comfortable with the plan and knowing they wouldn't get separated this way, Jesse set out again. He fell into the rhythm of their system: walking for a while, shouting back until he heard a response, and then walking again.

During one of these breaks, Jesse found a flat rock close to the river and sat down to rest. If he hadn't been lost in the woods with his injured friend, he might have even enjoyed the view. He yelled out again for Kevin, but still didn't hear an answer. Jesse let his mind wander for a bit, thinking about what he would do when they were rescued. Or rather, what he wanted to eat as soon as they were back to civilization. As he was zoning out, he saw something moving out of the corner of his eye. His heart skipped a beat, thinking it might be the wolf again. But it wasn't. He turned to look at the object moving in the river for a few seconds before realizing that it was a reflection of something.

A car!

There was a road running along the other side of the river. It wasn't the road they'd been aiming for, but Jesse would take anything he could get. He jumped up and down, waved his arms, and shouted at the top of his lungs—but the car didn't even slow down.

Think, he told himself. *How can I get someone in a car way over there to see me?*

The answer was they wouldn't, unless they happened to be looking into the woods as they were driving past. But he knew that the chances of that happening weren't good, and he didn't want to risk missing another car. He needed something to signal the people on the other side of the river. Maybe a mirror. Or he could tie the blanket from the emergency kit to a stick to make a big flag.

Jesse dug into his bag to see what else he could use. His heart flipped over when he saw his phone. If they were this close to a road, there was a good chance they'd be able to get a signal now. Maybe they didn't need to get a driver's attention after all.

He dug the phone out of the pack and pushed the button to wake it up. The screen stayed black. The battery was completely drained.

CHAPTER 12

"Do you have your phone?" Jesse asked as soon as Kevin came into view.

"Why are you waiting for me?" Kevin asked. "We agreed—"

"I saw a car," Jesse said before Kevin could finish complaining. "I saw a car and I tried to get their attention, but I couldn't. But maybe since we're so close to the road we can get a signal." He said it all in one breath and very fast. But Kevin seemed to understand enough.

Kevin found his own phone and started pushing buttons. "Dead," he declared. "We should have turned them off to save the batteries."

"It's too late to worry about that now," Jesse said. "We have to find some way of signaling across the river."

"What do you have in mind?"

Jesse shrugged. "I was hoping you would have an idea."

Kevin stared across the river. "How many cars have you seen go by?"

"Just one," Jesse told him.

"Then we should keep going," Kevin said. "We have no idea how busy that road is. We're better off pushing on until we find a road on this side of the river. It can't be too much farther now."

"I could swim across," Jesse suggested.

"No way," Kevin said. "Look at how wide the river is. The current looks super fast out toward the middle, and there's all kinds of logs and who knows what else floating downstream. It's too dangerous. Plus, I bet it's really cold too."

Jesse remembered how cold the river was when he went to fill their water bottle and shivered involuntarily. He would still risk the cold water if it meant getting them out of there, but he knew that Kevin would never agree to that plan. Jesse decided not to argue the point now and save it as a last resort.

"All right," he said at last. "We'd better get going then."

They set off again, with Jesse in the lead and Kevin falling behind faster than he had before. Jesse was getting very worried about his friend. Kevin was putting on a brave face, but there was no way Jesse should be getting so far ahead so quickly. Kevin was usually a much faster walker than Jesse. And Jesse was going slower than usual because of clearing the way for Kevin.

When Jesse came to a clearing with a good view of the other side of the river, he stopped again to let Kevin catch up. By the time he saw his friend limping into view several minutes later, Jesse had seen enough.

"You can't keep going like this," Jesse said.

"I'm fine," Kevin said.

"No, you're not. We need another plan. And I think I have one."

Kevin gave a sigh of defeat. "All right. Let's hear it."

"We'll build a fire," Jesse said. "A big fire over here would be sure to catch the attention of anyone driving past on the other side of the river. And if it gets dark, it will only be that much more obvious. At the very least they'll report the fire to the police and someone will come to put it out."

"What if no other cars come by tonight?" Kevin asked. "It's already getting dark. That could be a private road or something."

"I've thought about that," Jesse said. "After we get the fire going I'll keep walking. I'll stick to the river like we've been doing. That way we've got two ways of finding help. If someone sees the fire, you can send them along the river to find me. And if I get to a road, I'll tell them to look for the fire to find you."

Kevin screwed up his face like he was looking for flaws in Jesse's plan. "Okay," he said finally. "I don't really like being left behind, but . . ." Kevin broke off and winced. "I'm not sure how much farther I can go."

Jesse set to work finding all the dry twigs and logs he could get his hands on. He brought them back to Kevin who set up the fire. Jesse was grateful for Kevin's skills. The only fire *he* had ever started was in his fireplace at home. And that was gas.

After a short time, Kevin had the logs leaning against one another with smaller twigs along the outside. He'd even cleared a space around the setup to prevent the fire from spreading.

Jesse made several more trips to bring back armloads of sticks. He wanted Kevin to have a good supply of fuel before he left—enough to keep the fire going the whole night if needed.

Once Jesse was satisfied with the stack of wood piled up beside his friend, he sat down on the ground on the other side of the campfire setup. "This should be a good supply," Kevin said, nodding thoughtfully. "Of course, we still have to light it. If only we had some kind of glass, we could use it to focus the sun into a single spot. I guess we'll have to use friction. I can build something that will help me rub the sticks together until they get hot enough to light the tinder on fire."

Jesse dug the emergency kit out of Kevin's backpack and held up the box of matches. "Or we could use these," he said with a grin.

Kevin laughed. "You are brilliant," he said.

"I have my moments," Jesse said.

As soon as the fire was blazing, Jesse got up to go. Kevin awkwardly got to his feet, not even bothering to try to hide the pain now.

"Take care out there," he said.

"You too," Jesse said. Then he headed out into the unknown all alone.

CHAPTER
13

Jesse walked for what felt like hours. The sun was so low in the sky it was lost in the treetops and the darkness was closing in quickly. The air got colder as the light went away, and Jesse was soon shivering in his light windbreaker. He was glad Kevin had the fire to keep warm. Glad, and maybe a little jealous.

He stayed as close to the river as possible, but at times the trees were so thick he had to walk farther out. When he had a clear view across the river, he would look out to the road in hopes he might spot a car.

On one of his detours away from the shore he thought he heard a car. He pushed his way

through the trees and made it to the river
in time to see what might have been a car's
taillights in the distance. Or it could have just
been the setting sun reflecting off the road.

Please let that be a car, he thought. *And please
let the driver see the fire.*

But he couldn't count on that. He had to
keep going.

The moon was up in the dark red twilight
sky, and it twinkled off the river in weird ways.
It was getting harder to see the road on the
other side of the river. Jesse stopped to look. In
the darkness it seemed farther away. Then he
realized that was because the road was curving
away from the other shore of the river.

Jesse had been hoping that road would
cross the river on a bridge over to his side
so he could catch up to it there. That clearly
wasn't going to happen. He was starting to
lose hope that he would ever reach the road to
the south either.

If there even is a road to the south, Jesse
thought miserably. The longer he was out in
the woods, the less confident he was in how

well he knew the area. *Maybe the road on the other side of the river is the one I was thinking of and there's no way to reach it.*

A nagging thought in the back of his mind reminded Jesse that there *was* a way. Kevin had shot down Jesse's suggestion about swimming across the river when they'd first found the road. But the river was much narrower here, only about half as wide as before. Which probably meant the current wouldn't be as strong.

Jesse had no idea what to do. Kevin's concerns still played in his head, but their situation had only gotten worse, and the longer he waited, the slimmer the odds of finding a car once he got to the other side. He weighed his options and realized he didn't really have any. Kevin was hurt, and they needed to get help as soon as possible. He had to get across to that road, and he had to do it soon.

Jesse went to the edge of the water and stuck his hand in. It was colder than he remembered. He had taken swim lessons long enough to know it was risky to attempt to cross in such cold water. But he had to try.

Jesse took off his shoes and windbreaker. They would be too heavy and might drag him down once they were soaking wet. The air was cold, but he was going to be a whole lot colder in a minute.

Before Jesse took the plunge, he brought his things back to where he'd been walking. If Kevin was rescued and sent someone looking for him, they'd follow the trail of broken branches and find it. He didn't have a pen or anything to write on, so he arranged his windbreaker with one arm pointing toward the river. Then he put rocks on the sleeve and the other corners of the jacket to hold it in place. He left a trail of his belongings from the jacket to the shore just in case his first message wasn't clear.

No turning back now, Jesse told himself.

He stepped into the cold water and gave himself a minute to get used to the temperature. Then he took a few steps forward so the water was up to his knees, then his thighs, then his waist. By now he was shivering so badly his teeth were chattering, but he hoped easing his

way in would mean that the final dive wouldn't
be too much of a shock.

He was wrong.

He launched himself underwater headfirst
from his standing position, hoping to get
a little extra push before he had to start
swimming for real. The cold that surrounded
him stunned him for a moment. When he
came back up to the surface, he was unsure if
he would be able to move at all.

Get moving, he told himself. *Slow, steady
movements. Remember to breathe.*

He kicked his legs and pulled his arms
through the water one at a time. He turned his
head to breathe with every other stroke.

His body strained from the effort,
already tired. When he looked up he was
shocked to see he was only about a quarter
of the way across. The shore looked a
lot farther away than it had when he was
standing on dry land. He put his head back
down and tried to think of nothing but the
strokes pulling him forward as he cut
through the water.

Jesse didn't let himself look up again, but he could feel he'd made it to the middle, as the current was getting stronger. Much stronger. He tried not to fight against it, to keep himself pointed toward the shore and not worry about drifting downstream. But before long, Jesse was struggling just to keep his head above water.

Then something brushed against his leg.

Jesse let out a yell. Big mistake. Water filled
his mouth and nose. He gasped as he tried to
keep his head above the water long enough to
catch his breath. No matter what he did, water
kept going up his nose and down his throat.

Jesse forced himself to stop panicking
and concentrated on treading water until
he got his breath back. He peered through
the weak light of the moon and last rays of
the sun and saw sticks and leaves and garbage
floating all around him. Kevin had warned
him about this, but he hadn't realized how
much of a problem it would be. He started
swimming again, but now he kept his head

above the water, watching carefully to make sure nothing took him by surprise again.

Swimming like this was slower, and he was exhausted. He wasn't sure he had the strength to keep going for much longer. He saw a giant log coming down the river a little ways ahead of him and got an idea.

Jesse put on a burst of speed to get to where the log was going to cross in front of him. When it was in reach, he pushed himself forward and grabbed ahold of it. Using the log to keep his head above water, he could focus all of his energy on kicking and keeping himself headed toward the shore.

Jesse knew he could be stubborn. He knew it got in the way a lot of the time. But Jesse was going to use every bit of stubbornness in him to get to the other side of the river. There was no way he was going through all of this only to fail when he was so close.

When his arms grew tired, he held on tighter. When he felt short of breath, he forced his lungs to keep breathing. When he got a cramp in his leg, he kept kicking.

I will not fail, I will not fail, I will not fail.

Jesse was so focused on keeping his body going he was surprised when his feet touched the bottom a yard from the river's edge.

Jesse let go of the log and half-walked, half-swam the rest of the way. He crawled out of the water onto shore. Lying on his back, looking up at the starry sky, he sucked in several deep breaths of air. He was alive. But not safe. Not yet. He still had a long way to go. And Kevin was counting on him.

Jesse got to his feet and stumbled away from the shore, but his worst fears were soon confirmed. There was no sign of the road. He peered upstream through the quickly growing darkness, but there was no sign of Kevin's signal fire.

Jesse was colder than he'd ever been in his life. His muscles were stiff and sore from walking through the woods all day and then swimming across the river. He had no idea where he was, where Kevin was, or how he was going to find anyone to help them. It finally seemed that things really couldn't be worse.

He was so tired. But Jesse shuddered at the thought of what would happen if he stopped moving. So he stood, shivering but determined, and started walking.

CHAPTER
15

The last of the sun was gone now. Jesse
had to rely on the moonlight to find his
way through the thick undergrowth, which
was made even more challenging by his
lack of shoes. Sometimes the bushes and
roots were so thick that he was forced back
to the river to wade along the shore until
there was another break in the trees where
he could get back to dry land. Each detour
into the river left him colder and more tired
than before.

Jesse's body ached from cold and fatigue. It
took everything in his power to fight against
the desire to quit and lie down where he was.

He rubbed his arms to try to warm up, but it barely seemed to make a difference.

He was concentrating on the ground, staring at the spot right in front of him, willing himself to keep moving forward. Then something caught his attention: a little flicker far upstream across the river. Jesse strained his eyes and focused. It was the fire! Kevin must have built it up even more once the sun went down. Just seeing the flames sent a surge of warmth through Jesse's whole body.

Even better—if he could see the fire, that meant he was back to where the road was closer to the river. Jesse turned away from the river and walked inland. The ground sloped so steeply that he had to use tree branches and roots to pull himself up the last few feet, but once he made it up to the top, he was well rewarded.

Jesse had found the road! He'd done it. As soon as a car came by, they would be saved. He started walking again, following the road back toward where Kevin was so he would be as close as possible when he found someone to help them. As he walked, he kept an eye on the fire. Watching it grow larger gave him the motivation to keep going. It wouldn't be too long before he was right across the river from Kevin.

A new panic swept over Jesse. What if no cars came by before he reached the point across from Kevin's fire? He was too cold to sit down and wait, but too tired to walk much farther.

Then he heard it. The swish of tires on pavement. The low rumble of an engine getting steadily louder and closer.

Suddenly, Jesse realized he had no idea what to do. If he stood in the middle of the road, he risked getting hit. If he stayed on the side of the road, the driver might not see him at all. He needed some way to signal the driver while still keeping himself safe.

And he only had a few seconds left to decide what to do.

Jesse looked around wildly and saw a tree branch lying by the side of the road. It must have come down recently because the leaves were still thick and green. He picked it up and positioned himself on the edge of the road.

Light momentarily blinded Jesse as the car came around a bend and its headlights shone directly into his eyes. His heart beat faster. He shouted and jumped and waved the tree branch so it was halfway into the driver's lane. Even if the driver didn't see or hear him, the car would hit the branch and get the driver's attention that way.

For a second Jesse panicked as the car continued to speed along with no sign of braking. Then, tires screeched across the pavement and the car came to a stop just a couple of feet away. A man jumped out of the car.

"What in the world do you think you're doing?" he shouted. "You could have been killed!"

Jesse laughed. He could have been killed half a dozen times in the last twenty-four hours. This was probably one of the safer things he'd done. But once Jesse started laughing, he couldn't stop. He dropped the branch and sank to his knees. The laughter turned into sobs.

He cried with relief, and exhaustion, and fear, and more relief.

"Hey, buddy. It's okay," the man said. He came closer, and in the light of his headlights Jesse could see he was wearing well-worn, sturdy boots like Kevin's. A local. Someone who would actually be able to help.

"Please, help us," Jesse cried. "My friend . . ."

He couldn't get out any more words, but he didn't have to. The man went back to his car and returned with a thick wool blanket that he draped around Jesse as he helped him to his feet. It was scratchy and smelled like earth but it was the most wonderful thing Jesse had ever felt in his entire life.

"Now then," the man said. "My name is Buck. Everything is going to be all right. You get so your teeth aren't chattering, and then you tell me everything."

Jesse did. He told Buck about the traffic jam and the tree and getting stuck in the mud. He talked about the wolf and Kevin's wound. The words spilled out of him as he described his desperate decision to swim across the river.

"That was a really stupid thing to do," Buck said when Jesse was done. "But it's a good thing you did. That road you were looking for went out of commission when they rebuilt the main highway some years back. And the closest bridge is a good ten miles upstream."

Jesse looked across the river to where he could just barely make out the shape of Kevin sitting next to the fire. "I have to get back to my friend."

"Don't worry," Buck told him. "My friend Kristi lives a short way up the river and has a boat. She's the best hunter in this part of the woods. She'll have no trouble finding your friend with that fire going like it is."

Jesse sat in the car with the heat on full blast while Buck called his friend. In what seemed like no time at all, a boat came down the river and pulled up to the opposite shore. In a couple of minutes, the fire went out and then the boat's engine roared back to life.

Buck drove Jesse to Kristi's house. When they arrived, Kevin was already there, waiting for them.

"You did it!" Kevin said, clapping Jesse on the back.

"We did it," Jesse corrected. "Together."

Buck and Kristi made them sandwiches as the boys called home using Kristi's phone.

"Was your dad upset about the car?" Kevin asked when Jesse got off the phone.

Jesse shook his head. "They were worried when we didn't check in last night. I guess they had enough time to get scared that something happened to me that they don't even care about the car."

"See?" Kevin grinned at Jesse in an I-told-you-so kind of way.

"Do you always have to be so stubborn?" Jesse asked.

They both laughed.

It didn't take long before their families got there. Jesse's mom and dad and Kevin's dads had gone to the cabin that morning and spent the rest of the day looking for the boys, so they were close by. They all insisted on hearing the whole story before taking the boys home. Jesse and Kevin told it in turns, and when they were done, both sets of parents hugged both boys.

"So, any chance you'd like to hang out again next weekend?" Jesse asked as they walked to their cars.

"Of course," Kevin said. "But next time let's try something a little less dangerous. Ever been cliff diving?"

ABOUT THE AUTHOR

Jannette LaRoche is a librarian in the Quad Cities, Illinois. She has been working with teens for over eighteen years and is passionate about getting the right book into the hands of the right reader at the right time. She is especially interested in connecting teens who don't consider themselves readers with stories that will help them fall in love with books. She holds a BA in English, an MS in library science, and an MFA in creative writing.

ROAD
TRIP

HEAT WAVE

OFF COURSE

SPINNING OUT

STRANDED

DAY OF DISASTER

AFTERSHOCK

BACKFIRE

BLACK BLIZZARD

DEEP FREEZE

VORTEX

WALL OF WATER

Would you survive?

ATTACK ON EARTH

WHEN ALIENS INVADE,
ALL YOU CAN DO IS SURVIVE.

DESERTED

THE FALLOUT

THE FIELD TRIP

GETTING HOME

LOCKDOWN

TAKE SHELTER

CHECK OUT ALL THE TITLES IN THE
ATTACK ON EARTH SERIES

MASON FALLS MYSTERIES

EVEN AN ORDINARY TOWN HAS ITS SECRETS.